MY BROWN BEAR BARNEY

By Dorothy Butler
Illustrated by Elizabeth Fuller

GREENWILLOW BOOKS, NEW YORK

Library of Congress Cataloging-in-Publication Data
Butler, Dorothy (date)
My brown bear Barney/ by Dorothy Butler;
illustrated by Elizabeth Fuller.
p.   cm.
Summary: On her many travels,
a small girl takes many things,
especially her brown bear Barney.
ISBN 0-688-08567-9.
ISBN 0-688-08568-7 (lib. bdg.)
[1. Teddy bears—Fiction.]
I. Fuller, Elizabeth (Elizabeth A.), ill.
II. Title.   PZ7.B976My 1989
[E]—dc19   88-21199   CIP   AC

When I go shopping, I take . . .

my mother, my little brother, my yellow basket,
my red umbrella

and my brown bear Barney.

When I play with my friend Fred,
I take . . .

my bike, our old dog Charlie, two apples from our tree,
my boots

and my brown bear Barney.

When I go gardening, I take . . .

my father, my straw hat, my wheelbarrow, my spade

and my brown bear Barney.

When I go to the beach, I take . . .

my mother, my father, my little brother, special things to eat,
my sunglasses

and my brown bear Barney.

When I go to my grandmother's,
I take . . .

my pajamas in a suitcase, a flower in green paper,
a tasty tidbit for her cat, some carrots from my garden

and my brown bear Barney.

When I go to bed, I take . . .

a good book or two, our old dog Charlie,
an apple for the morning, my big silver flashlight

and my brown bear Barney.

When I go to school, next year or the next,
I'll take . . .

a new school bag, some lunch, my dinosaur badge and
a pencil with an eraser on the end.

But not my brown bear Barney.
My mother says that bears don't go to school.

We'll see about that!